Little Big Sister

Rachel Pank

for Sarah

First published in hardback and in Collins Toddler in
Great Britain by HarperCollins Publishers Ltd in 1996.
First published in Picture Lions in 1999.

1 3 5 7 9 10 8 6 4 2

ISBN 0 00 664697-2

Picture Lions is an imprint of the Children's Division,
part of HarperCollins Publishers Ltd.

Printed and bound by Imago.

Little Big Sister

Rachel Pank

Picture Lions
An Imprint of HarperCollins*Publishers*

This is little Lottie and her
big sister Kate.
Kate says that because
she's nearly four she wants
to be grown-up.

Lottie wonders what Kate will do.
She follows her upstairs and into
Mummy and Daddy's bedroom.

"Those are Mummy's clothes,"
says Lottie.

Kate tries on a flowery dress.

Lottie helps Kate
do her hair.

She chooses some
shoes for Kate.

Kate puts on dingley dangley
earrings, bangles, necklaces
and a brooch.

And then the best bit of all,
Kate puts on her make-up.
Lottie just can't wait to help.

Pink lipstick and cream. Perfume and powder. Purple eye pencil.

"Let me," says Lottie.

"Shh!" whispers Kate,
"Mummy's coming!"

"Kate," cries Mummy,
"what are you doing?"

"Off with my clothes!"
"But Mum..." says Kate.
"Off with my shoes
and into the bath!"

"But I only wanted to be grown-up."

When Kate is clean and dry
she goes to her room.

What is Lottie doing there?

She's trying on Kate's clothes!

"Off with my clothes!"
"But Kate..."
"Off with my shoes!"

"But I only wanted to be grown-up.
I want to be like YOU!" Lottie shouts.

"Do you really think I'm grown-up?"

"Of course you're grown-up,"
Lottie says, "because...

you're my BIG sister!"